This book belongs to

NICO WILLIAMS

CARLTON
KIDS

This is a Carlton Book

Published in 2016 by Carlton Books Ltd,
an imprint of the Carlton Publishing Group,
20 Mortimer Street, London W1T 3JW

Design and text copyright © 2016 Carlton Books Ltd
Illustrations © Patricia Moffett 2009, 2016

ISBN: 978-1-78312-219-6

Printed in China

Executive Editor: Bryony Davies
Editor: Anna Brett
Creative Director: Clare Baggaley
Designer: Alison Tutton

FAIRIES
A Spotter's Handbook

ILLUSTRATED BY
PATRICIA MOFFETT

ALISON
MALONEY

CONTENTS

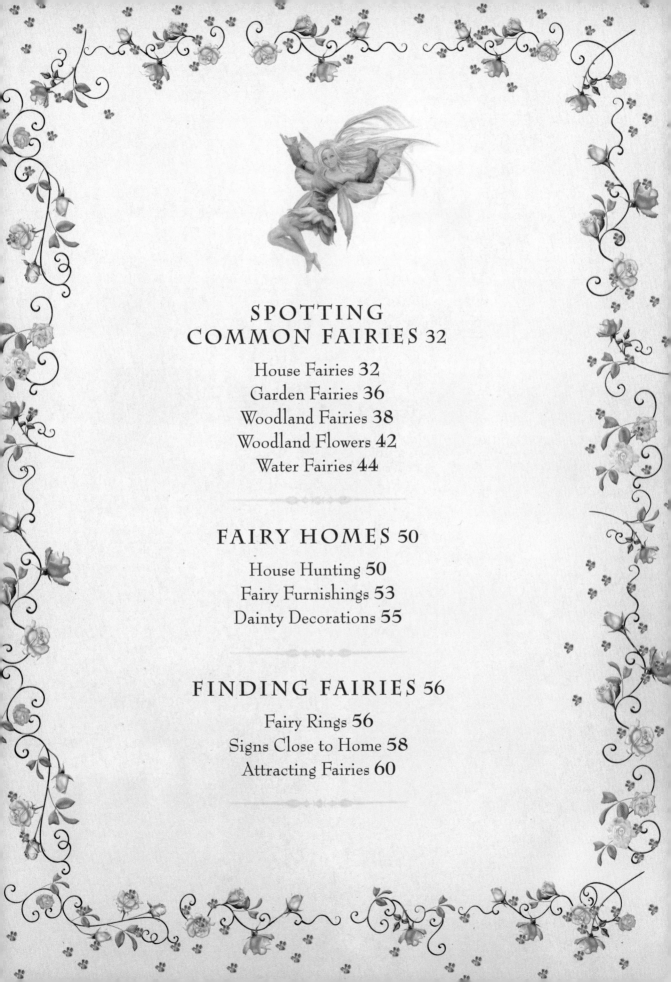

WELCOME TO FAIRYLAND

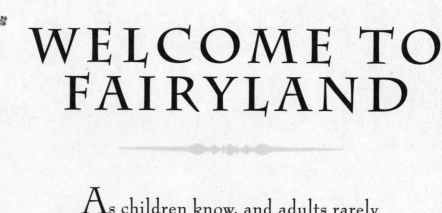

As children know, and adults rarely understand, fairies are everywhere – in gardens, the woods beyond and even in your house! Although fairies can be found in every country in the mortal world, their true home is the far-off kingdom of Fairyland. In order to be a successful fairy spotter, you must first understand their world and how they live their lives.

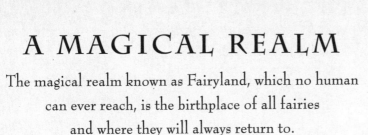

A MAGICAL REALM

The magical realm known as Fairyland, which no human
can ever reach, is the birthplace of all fairies
and where they will always return to.

Fairyland looks quite different from our world. The
sky can change from blue to green in an instant, and
the clouds look like candy floss. The streams and rivers
run with shimmering gold, and the lakes contain pure
dew water. Flowers of every description can be found
throughout Fairyland – from roses and violets, to
fantastical creations of silver and gold.

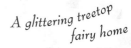

*A glittering treetop
fairy home*

In Fairyland, pixies sell food, clothes and shoes alongside
fairy dust, wands and ingredients for magic spells. Stores
are bursting with honey, dew-drop drinks and fruit, and
they stock more herbs than you have ever heard of, with
strange names like Mouse-ear Hawkweed, Hog's Fennel
and Squirting Cucumber.

Fairies use fairy gold for money, but beware
the fairy that tries to sneak some out of Fairyland –
it will instantly turn to dry leaves!

A magical fairy meeting place

A pixie shop

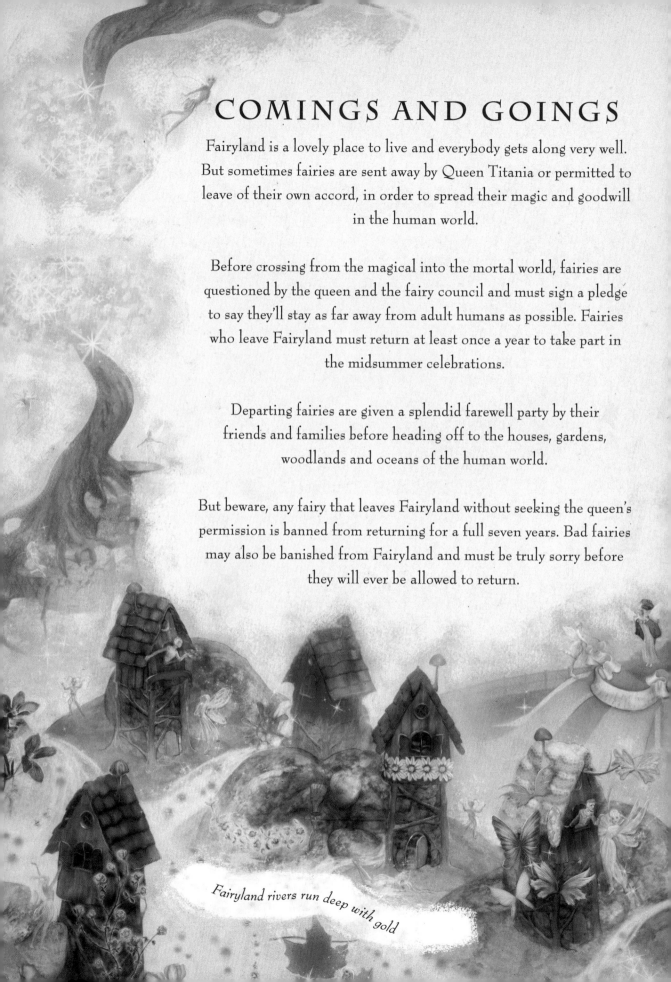

COMINGS AND GOINGS

Fairyland is a lovely place to live and everybody gets along very well. But sometimes fairies are sent away by Queen Titania or permitted to leave of their own accord, in order to spread their magic and goodwill in the human world.

Before crossing from the magical into the mortal world, fairies are questioned by the queen and the fairy council and must sign a pledge to say they'll stay as far away from adult humans as possible. Fairies who leave Fairyland must return at least once a year to take part in the midsummer celebrations.

Departing fairies are given a splendid farewell party by their friends and families before heading off to the houses, gardens, woodlands and oceans of the human world.

But beware, any fairy that leaves Fairyland without seeking the queen's permission is banned from returning for a full seven years. Bad fairies may also be banished from Fairyland and must be truly sorry before they will ever be allowed to return.

Fairyland rivers run deep with gold

Fairy palace

A flower fairy

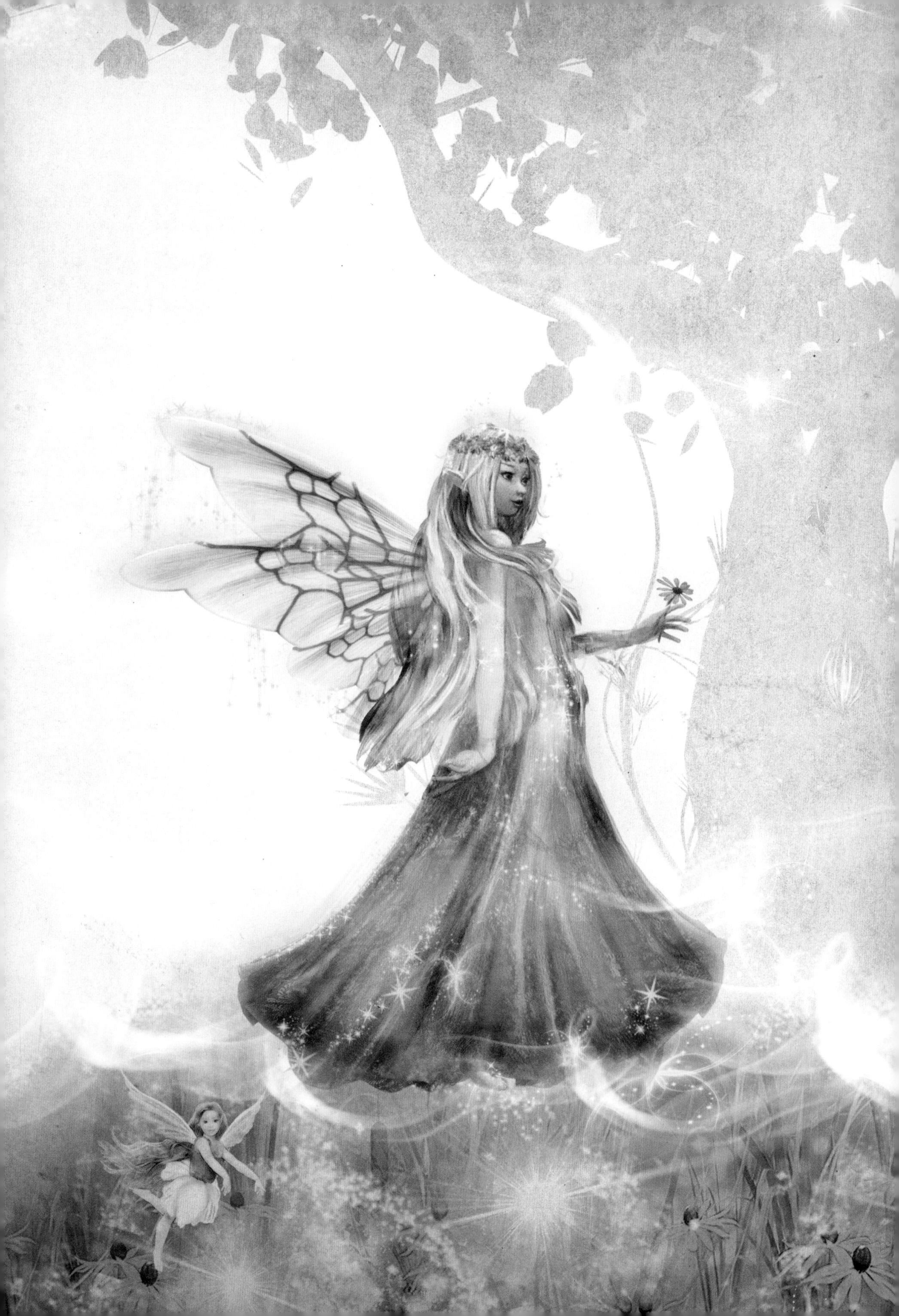

THE RULES OF FAIRYLAND

All fairies must obey these rules in order to live
together in harmony and happiness.

* A fairy must always be considerate towards
his or her fellow citizens.
* Deliberate damage to property or nature's
treasures will not be tolerated.
* Animals are our friends and cruelty to them is an offence.
* Jeering, mocking and bullying others because of their
pointed ears, large nose or flat feet is strictly forbidden.
* Litter should never be dropped in the streets and
must be recycled in every instance.
* Any item stolen by a resident will instantly turn to dust.
* Tricks played on friends and neighbours must
be merely mischievous, never malicious.
* Fairies who leave the kingdom must return for the summer
festivities, or they will be unable to return for seven full years.
* Returning fairies must NEVER lead
a human to Fairyland.
* The queen must be obeyed at all times.

THE FAIRY
QUEEN'S CASTLE

On top of a steep hill, overlooking all of
Fairyland, stands a magnificent fairy castle.
Here lives Titania, queen of the fairies, and
her husband Oberon, the fairy king.

Beautiful and graceful, Titania is attended
by her flower-fairy maids.
She is kind and fair to her subjects, who
are always welcome at the castle.

ORCHESTRA →

FAIRY
GONDOLA

TITANIA'S
HORSE-DRAWN
COACH

15

Titania is dressed by flower-fairy maids every day.

LIFE AT THE CASTLE

Queen Titania likes nothing better than a good party so the ballroom is often in use! The highlight is the Midsummer Ball, when the sweetest nectar and honey are flown in by bees from all over the land, and the juiciest berries are served on tables around the room for everyone to enjoy.

When they can eat no more, the fairies dance by the light of the moon in the castle gardens, often until daybreak.

A royal child in the nursery

Titania's throne room

Fairies are always dancing at the castle.

Fairies that visit the castle do so in their most
exquisite gowns and finery. Titania has her gowns
sewn by the most experienced silkworms and they
seem to sparkle from every angle.

Everyone knows fairies can fly, but Titania likes to
encourage her guests to relax and be transported
around in style when visiting the castle. Royal
gondolas float along the streams and rivers in the
castle grounds and are a favourite pastime
for young visitors.

When leaving the castle to visit her subjects in
faraway corners of Fairyland, Titania
travels in her grand golden coach.

FAMOUS FAIRIES

Some fairies are known throughout the magical and mortal worlds. They have made their way into stories that humans have told for generations. Understanding that these tales are true is important for anyone who wants to become a fairy spotter.

FAIRIES FROM FICTION

THE BLUE FAIRY

If it wasn't for the beautiful Blue Fairy, Pinocchio, a mischievous little puppet, would never have become a real boy!

SLEEPING BEAUTY'S FAIRIES

Sleeping Beauty had six fairy godmothers who tried
to protect her from their sister, the wicked fairy. The
wicked fairy cast a spell saying Sleeping Beauty would
prick her finger on her sixteenth birthday, and die.
However, one of the good fairies used her magic to
soften the curse so that the princess wouldn't die but
instead fall into a deep sleep that would last for a
hundred years. Sure enough, these things came to pass,
but after a hundred years a handsome prince was able to
rouse the princess with a gentle kiss!

THUMBELINA
AND TOM THUMB

Thumbelina was a beautiful, tiny fairy child who emerged from a flower and was brought up by a human woman. Kidnapped by a frog who wanted a bride for her son, Thumbelina escaped with the help of a butterfly, but was then stolen away by a mayfly! After many adventures Thumbelina was finally delivered to a handsome fairy prince on the back of a bird.

Like Thumbelina, Tom Thumb was a fairy child, no bigger than a thumb, who was raised by human parents. He was very accident-prone and often fell into animal troughs and pots, but he used his fairy magic to escape each danger.

TINKER BELL

The most famous fairy of all, Tinker Bell, was Peter Pan's
own fairy. She was given her name because she fixed pots and
kettles, like a tinker, and her voice sounded like a bell. Tinker
Bell was no bigger than a hand but she was very beautiful. She
flitted around very fast and appeared as a tiny light in the dark.
She could be very bad-tempered, but was devoted to Peter and
protected him from the evil Captain Hook.

Tinker Bell lived in a place called Neverland and shared her
home with the Lost Boys, a group of children who never grew
up. Pirates, mermaids and Red Indians also lived in Neverland,
which can only be reached by flying past a certain star.

THE SNOW QUEEN

Long ago in a cold land, far far away, lived a boy named Kay and his best friend Gerda. Kay's grandmother often told the two children stories of a fairy queen who lived in the ice realm and ruled over the 'snow bees', tiny creatures that travelled around the world with the snow. She was extraordinarily beautiful and graceful, but anyone who was kissed by her three times instantly turned to ice.

One day, an evil troll broke a magic mirror that splintered into a million tiny pieces and scattered to the ends of the earth. A tiny splinter lodged in Kay's heart, turning it to ice, and another in his eye, meaning he could only see bad and ugly things. He began to turn mean and nasty towards Gerda and they fought for the first time.

One cold, snowy night the Snow Queen appeared and beckoned to Kay, who couldn't resist climbing on her sledge. The fairy queen kissed him twice to make him forget all about his grandmother and Gerda, and then she whisked him away to her magnificent ice palace.

Kay's grandmother sat at home and wept, believing the boy had drowned in the river, but Gerda was sure she could find him. She travelled for miles, meeting many magical people who helped her on the way, and finally a reindeer took her to the ice palace where she found Kay.

Although the walls of the Snow Queen's palace were made of ice, Kay could feel no cold, as his heart had frozen. When Gerda entered the palace, Kay was so still she thought he had been turned to ice forever. She hugged him and wept, and her hot tears melted his heart. He looked at Gerda and started to cry, and his own tears washed away the piece of mirror in his eye. Instantly, he recognized his friend and cried, "Gerda, where have you been? Where have I been?"

Hand in hand, Gerda and Kay travelled back to their village and to Kay's grandmother, who was overjoyed to see them.

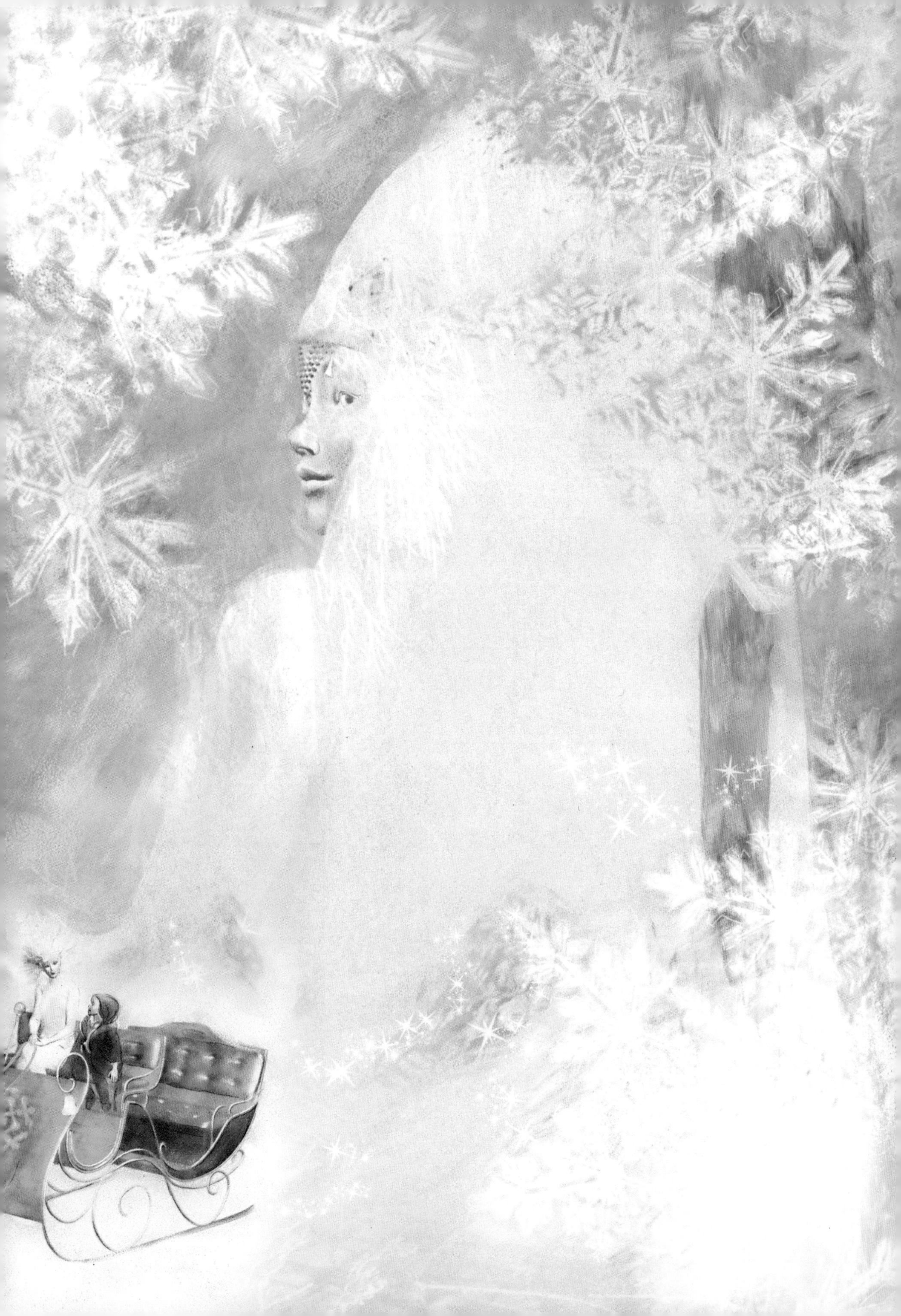

FAIRIES AND HUMANS

Some types of fairies are famous because of the way they interact with humans once in the mortal realm. They can be loving and giving – or not, in the case of the changelings! Be wary of fairies that make themselves known to humans in obvious ways – remember that good fairies must pledge to stay away from adults if they are allowed to leave Fairyland with the queen's blessing!

FAIRY GODMOTHERS

Most children have a fairy godmother to watch over them, although they are rarely seen. Cinderella was lucky enough to meet hers when she was in desperate need of help, otherwise she would never have made it to the ball. Sleeping Beauty was even luckier – her six fairy godmothers made sure the wicked fairy didn't get her way! If you should come across your fairy godmother, make the most of it. They are only given power to help each person once, so make sure you ask for the right favour!

CHANGELINGS

Changelings are fairy children that have been left in the place of human babies so that the fairies may have a human servant. Changelings are usually bad-tempered, with a face which looks a bit like an old man or woman, and they are exceptionally irritating. The only way of finding out whether your brother or sister is a changeling is to serve them dinner in an eggshell. If they are bad fairies they will cackle like an old man and speak as though they have lived for a hundred years. But don't worry, changelings are extremely rare!

FAIRY MAGIC

Fairies are magical creatures. In order to spot them you'll have to be clever as they can use their magic to avoid human sight. Read up on the methods they use to cast their spells and you'll recognize the signs of a nearby fairy.

MAGIC WANDS

Not all fairies carry wands but those that do are very careful never to lose them, as they can be dangerous in the wrong hands. The perfect wand is made from a hazel stick. It is whittled, which means the bark is cut away, and then a sparkling crystal is tied to the end. The wand is sprinkled with fairy dust to give it special powers. A fairy always writes her name, in invisible letters that only she can read, on the wood.

FAIRY DUST

A fairy will never travel without a special pouch of fairy dust. The ingredients are a secret that only the fairy king and queen are allowed to know, but it is thought that the dust falls from the moon and stars at night. Fairy dust contains so much magic that a fairy's spell will work on anything the dust touches. This does mean that they have to be very careful where it lands!

FAIRY ARROWS

Arrows, or elf-bolts, are made from tiny pieces of flint and can be used by both good and bad fairies. They were once used by the woodland fairies to scare off hunters, but today they are used to deliver love potions or fairy medicine to needy humans. Some wicked fairies use them to make farm animals sick if a farmer has offended them.

FOUR-LEAF CLOVER

These tiny plants are extremely rare and very precious to fairies as they can be used to ward off bad spells. Humans consider them lucky too, so keep an eye out for one and a fairy might be nearby! The first leaf is said to bring hope, the second, faith and the third, love. The fourth leaf is for good luck.

FAIRY OINTMENT

This is a mysterious potion that fairies apply to the eyes of their newborn babies. It helps them to see magic which is never revealed to human eyes.

Fairy Spells

Magic can't happen without an accompanying spell. Young fairies inherit a spellbook from their grandparents and will add new spells to it over the years. The book is usually teeny tiny and some spells are written in invisible letters, but humans have been known to find these books hidden under a blade of grass, so be sure to keep your eyes open.

The spells on the next few pages are taken from a fairy spellbook discovered by a human. They have been adapted for human use, so why not give them a try?

A word of warning – if a nearby fairy recognizes your words, they may come close to investigate. But bad sometimes follows good so be careful who you attract.

A Spell to Bless Your Home

To bring good fairy magic to your home and keep the mischievous sprites away, put a sprig of rosemary or thyme near your front door, then repeat this spell twice:

We've rosemary, thyme and sweet-smelling flowers,
Good fairies can enjoy,
To this clear house that we call ours,
Bring love and peace and joy.

Fairy House Spell

If you want fairies to move into your garden and have built them a fairy house, then this spell can help to catch their attention. Stand by the fairy house at dusk and repeat this spell four times:

Fear not the goblin, sprite or gnome,
Good fairy make this house your home!

Bad Mood Spell

If you've woken up in a bit of a grump, and need some cheering up, find the prettiest flower in your garden and smell it. Then repeat this spell three times:

Happy sprites and joyful imps,
Bring nature's play to rest,
Banish black and moody thoughts,
So I might be my best.

Sleeping Spell

Try this spell to banish nightmares and replace them with sweet dreams. Lavender, in a cotton sachet, or a drop of lavender water on your pillow, attracts the dream fairies. Say this rhyme three times before going to sleep:

Dream fairies, fair and wild,
Bring happy sleep upon this child,
Sprinkle dust and purest dew,
And make my dreams as sweet as you!

Missing Belongings Spell

If you've lost something, close your eyes, remember the object
you have mislaid, and say:

Silkies, elves and brownies too,
Search north, south, east and west,
Search up and down and round and round,
And help me with my quest.

Hopefully, the place where you left the object will
pop into your thoughts!

Friendship Spell

To make sure friendships last forever, collect some fallen
petals or leaves, and give them to each of the friends you
want to stay close to. Then hold hands with your friends
and repeat this spell twice:

Oh fairies of the flower and tree,
Oh sprites of river, brook and sea,
Use your charms so we may be,
Friends throughout eternity.

SPOTTING COMMON FAIRIES

Now you understand the world that fairies inhabit and the way they live their lives, you can use your knowledge to start spotting fairies. But how will you identify what type of fairy it is that you spot? Use this guide to first identify the group and then the specific type.

HOUSE FAIRIES

Amongst all fairies, the group known as house fairies are probably the most useful to humans. As in all fairy domains, there are those who are naughty and unhelpful, but, for the most part, house fairies help with chores and look after the family. One thing these fairies have in common is the love of a clean house! They also need to be treated well – insult one and things could start to go wrong around the home...

FAIRY HOUSEKEEPER

This friendly fairy helps to manage the housework and watches over the family. Each house will only have one fairy housekeeper, and they instruct brownies and silkies in their work. This fairy loves children and will often choose a warm, loving home to stay in, particularly if the adults are tired and overworked. As well as helping with the cleaning, the fairy housekeeper will tuck children in and close windows if they are cold. She loves strawberries and cream, and will be delighted if you leave these out as a gift.

SILKIES

Silkies are pretty fairies who dress in white or grey silk dresses. In the old days, when people had servants to do their chores, silkies would scold those who were not doing a good job. Nowadays, silkies will do the chores themselves to help families who are too busy to clean properly. They can be very useful to forgetful people too, as they like to lead them to lost items such as keys or documents. However, they have a mischievous side and like to amuse themselves by jumping out of trees and scaring travellers!

PORTUNES

These tiny fairies look like wrinkled old men! They are so small they can get through locked doors and appear in farmhouses at night to roast frogs on the fire. They have been known to annoy people by leading horses into marshes and bogs.

BROWNIES

These cheerful little sprites are endlessly helpful and love to do housework. They are not the prettiest of creatures, with flat faces and lots of hair, but they have the most enchanting smiles and friendly characters. They love to play with children and any child lucky enough to meet a brownie will be entertained with wonderful stories. The only thing that will drive your brownie away is a gift left out for them. This insults their good nature and they will never return, so beware!

BOGGARTS

The boggart is not a welcome visitor in any home. Dirty and smelly gnome-like creatures, they wear wrinkled and dusty clothing. Extremely bad tempered, these fairies like playing nasty tricks, such as tipping over jugs and loudly slamming doors! Other favourite activities include tormenting dogs to make them bark and pulling the tails of cats. They are difficult to get rid of once they have moved in, but this can be done by making annoying noises such as banging pots and singing loudly.

FARMHAND FAIRIES

If you are lucky enough to live on a farm, you might encounter a farmhand fairy. These travelling fairies go from farm to farm, helping tend animals and crops. They often stop at the farmhouse door, asking for a glass of milk.

GARDEN FAIRIES

Of all the world's fairies, those found at the bottom
of your garden tend to be the smallest. Their tiny size
means that they can live close to humans – grown-
ups are usually too busy to spot these tiny gardeners
flitting about the flowerbeds. On the rare occasions
they are spotted, it is usually by a child. After all,
children take more notice of these things!

FLOWER FAIRIES

Fairies that tend the garden flowers are busy workers and wake
very early in the morning to make sure that the plants have
had enough dew. They check that buds and blooms are coming
through in the right colours, and can change them with fairy
dust if they aren't quite right. They are incredibly beautiful and
dress in delicate outfits made from fallen
petals and leaves.

PIXIES

Pixies are tiny winged creatures with pointed noses and ears,
and they are extremely friendly and helpful around the garden.
However, they enjoy playing pranks on humans, such as hiding
trowels and making plants grow in funny directions! Pixies love to
dance and often gather together at pixie fairs. You can sometimes
tell where they have met – they might leave behind a shimmering
footprint, made from pixie dust.

WOODLAND FAIRIES

Forests and woods are perfect places for shy little fairy folk to hide, and they are happiest living in unspoilt natural surroundings. Here, they are safe from the litter and noise of the human world, and from mortal eyes, especially those of grown-ups.

Woodland fairies enjoy each other's company and love to get together to share secrets and gossip! At night they gather to talk and dance, often at a spot with a circle of toadstools which is known as a fairy ring.

WOODLAND SPRITES

Sprites love water and are usually found near a stream or lake. They can be mischievous and enjoy teasing butterflies, but they are not spiteful. In the autumn, it is their job to paint the leaves different shades of yellow and red.

BUTTERFLY FAIRIES

Beautiful and extremely rare, these fairies have the coloured wings of butterflies. They live deep in the forest, and feed on flower nectar and honey. They are so shy, they are hardly ever spotted.

WOOD NYMPHS

These fairies live in trees and will only stay alive as long as their tree does. They are very beautiful and kind but will get angry if their homes are damaged. They love to see children climbing and having fun with trees, but do make sure you never break off a branch!

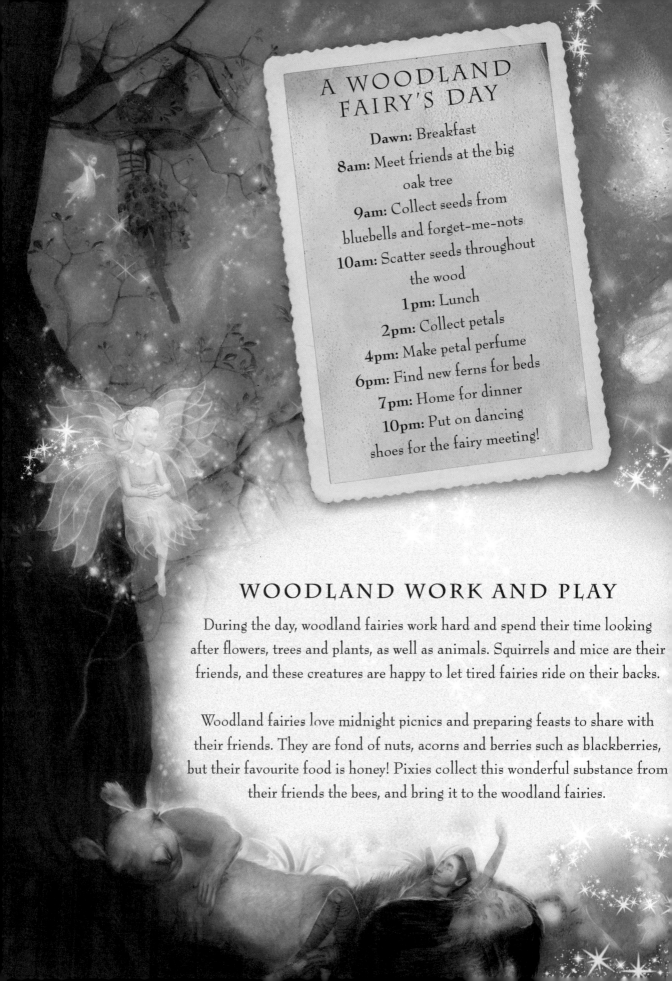

A WOODLAND FAIRY'S DAY

Dawn: Breakfast
8am: Meet friends at the big oak tree
9am: Collect seeds from bluebells and forget-me-nots
10am: Scatter seeds throughout the wood
1pm: Lunch
2pm: Collect petals
4pm: Make petal perfume
6pm: Find new ferns for beds
7pm: Home for dinner
10pm: Put on dancing shoes for the fairy meeting!

WOODLAND WORK AND PLAY

During the day, woodland fairies work hard and spend their time looking after flowers, trees and plants, as well as animals. Squirrels and mice are their friends, and these creatures are happy to let tired fairies ride on their backs.

Woodland fairies love midnight picnics and preparing feasts to share with their friends. They are fond of nuts, acorns and berries such as blackberries, but their favourite food is honey! Pixies collect this wonderful substance from their friends the bees, and bring it to the woodland fairies.

THE BLUEBELL
FESTIVAL

The most important day in the woodland fairy
calendar is the Bluebell Festival, which is
held in spring when the bluebells bloom. The
beautiful carpet of flowers provides a lovely
setting for this magical fairy festival, and the
little folk gather from miles around to celebrate.
Hundreds of fairies, in shimmering dresses and
their best waistcoats, dance throughout the night
to mark the end of the long, hard winter.

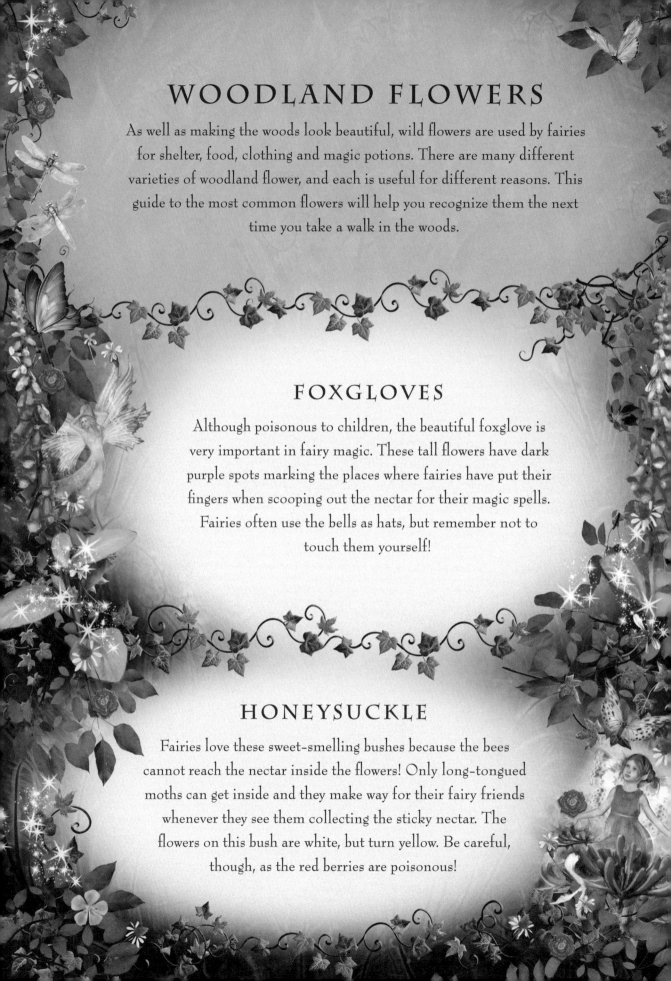

WOODLAND FLOWERS

As well as making the woods look beautiful, wild flowers are used by fairies for shelter, food, clothing and magic potions. There are many different varieties of woodland flower, and each is useful for different reasons. This guide to the most common flowers will help you recognize them the next time you take a walk in the woods.

FOXGLOVES

Although poisonous to children, the beautiful foxglove is very important in fairy magic. These tall flowers have dark purple spots marking the places where fairies have put their fingers when scooping out the nectar for their magic spells. Fairies often use the bells as hats, but remember not to touch them yourself!

HONEYSUCKLE

Fairies love these sweet-smelling bushes because the bees cannot reach the nectar inside the flowers! Only long-tongued moths can get inside and they make way for their fairy friends whenever they see them collecting the sticky nectar. The flowers on this bush are white, but turn yellow. Be careful, though, as the red berries are poisonous!

BLUEBELLS

A bluebell-covered wood is breathtakingly
beautiful and these flowers are a firm fairy
favourite. They bloom in spring and have
four or five purple-blue bells on each stem.

SNOWDROPS

Even before the bluebells carpet the woodlands,
the snowdrop brings news that winter is finally
over. As one of the first signs of spring, these
beautiful white flowers with their delicate
hanging heads are a sign of passing sorrow, and
the fairies rejoice when they see them.

FORGET-ME-NOTS

These are tiny blue and pink flowers which grow
in damp places, such as near a river, in the early
summer. They are called forget-me-nots for a good
reason – the fairies use their tiny petals to write
important messages to their friends.

WATER FAIRIES

Water has magical qualities and attracts many types of
fairy. Whether they live in vast seas, tranquil lakes or
tiny streams, the water fairies look after the plants, fish
and many other creatures that share
their underwater homes.

THE FIN FOLK

The Fin Folk, or Sea Gardeners, are tiny pixies who live in their own underwater paradise. They live mostly under the seas and oceans around the world, but are sometimes found in lagoons and saltwater lakes.

Gardening is the Fin Folk's favourite pastime and their kingdoms are full of brightly coloured flowers. These hardworking fairies spend all their waking hours tending to the plants and wildlife of the water, and have special spells to protect them. Fin Folk can grow flowers of colours never seen in the gardens of the human world, such as silver and gold. They have even grown a rainbow rose, which has petals in the seven colours of the rainbow!

Only a few lucky people have ever caught sight of these beautiful underwater realms – a magical sight that is never forgotten!

WATER SPRITES

These tiny fairies look like female humans, but have
hair as blue as the sea in which they live. They are able
to breathe in both air and water, and are friendly unless
threatened. They are happy to help humans in danger,
and have been known to rescue fishermen who have
fallen overboard.

THE LADY OF THE LAKE

You may have heard of King Arthur and his famous sword, Excalibur.
It was given to him by the fairy Queen Viviane, also known as the
Lady of the Lake. A water fairy with vast powers, the Lady of the Lake
gave the king the enchanted sword to protect him in battle. When he
was finally wounded, Excalibur was thrown back into the misty waters
and the Lady was seen rising above the water to reclaim it.

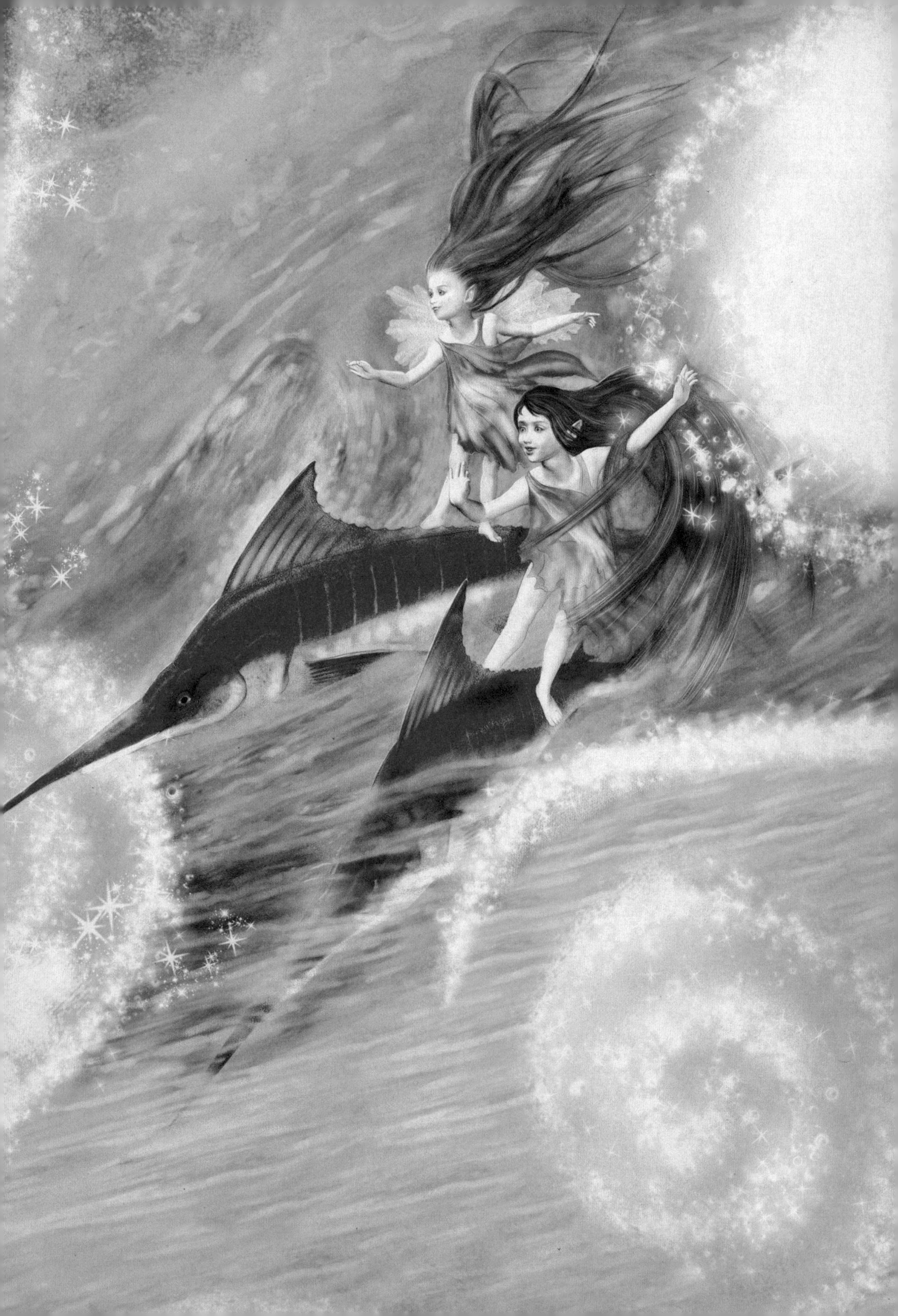

ASRAI

Small and beautiful, Asrai fairies are hard to spot as they are afraid of sunlight and are so delicate you can see right through them! They live in the deep blue seas and only come to the surface on moonless nights, once every hundred years.

THE FISHERMAN AND THE ASRAI

Long ago, when a full moon shone bright, a fisherman pulled in his nets to find a beautiful creature caught in the mesh. The Asrai begged him to release her, but her voice sounded like the waves, and he didn't hear. She pleaded with her eyes, but the fisherman was greedy, and thought he could make money from this wondrous creature.

When he reached the shore, the fisherman gathered the townsfolk together to take a look at his beautiful captive. However, when he moved the net, all he found was a puddle of water. He thought that perhaps he had dreamed everything. But, as the years went by, and whatever the weather, a spot on his arm where the Asrai had touched him remained icy cold.

WATER NYMPHS

Beautiful water nymphs watch over fountains, springs, wells and streams. Each
nymph stays with her own spring or stream, nourishing the surrounding land and
crops, and helping plants to grow. These fairies can give water special healing
powers. Those who drink from a fountain or well which is home to a water nymph
will soon find that good luck comes their way!

FAIRY HOMES

Fairies choose their homes very carefully.
For those who live in Fairyland, there is no problem
finding the perfect home. However, for garden,
woodland and water fairies, it can be difficult
finding the ideal abode. If you wish to spot a fairy at
home, look for the signs. You could even encourage
a fairy to inhabit a space you have created for them!

HOUSE HUNTING

Fairy homes need to be in a pretty setting hidden away from
inquisitive human eyes. They are always built in sheltered areas,
as fairies prefer not to get wet (unless they are water fairies, of
course!). Above all, the places they choose must be clean, as
fairies hate dirt and litter. Many a fairy has been forced to leave
their home because of careless litterbugs.

Garden fairies often build a tiny home from twigs and leaves.
Woodland fairies prefer the hollow of a tree, or the inside of
a very large toadstool. If you are lucky, you might find a fairy
ring, which is a circle of toadstools, used by the tiniest woodland
fairies who like to live together.

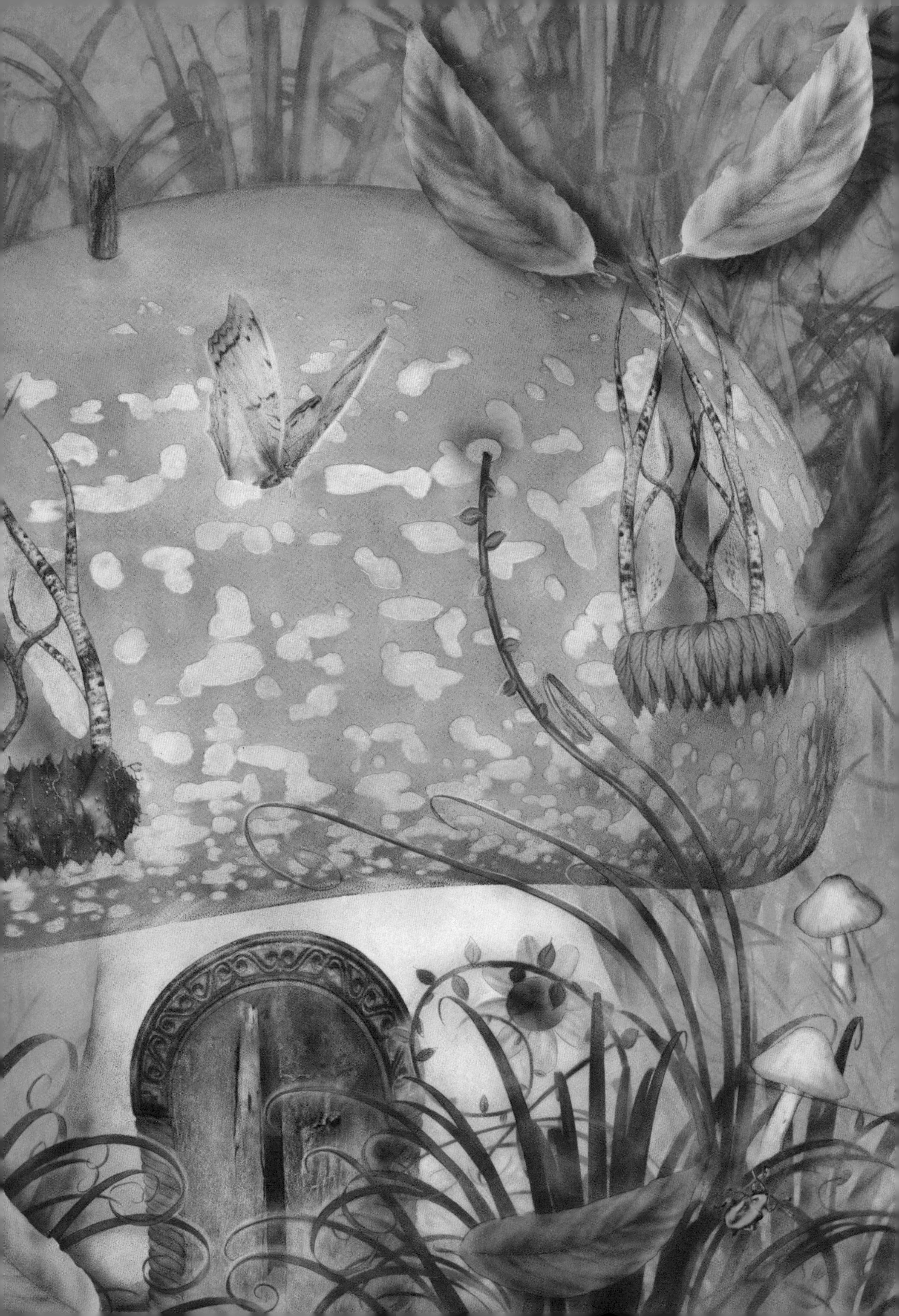

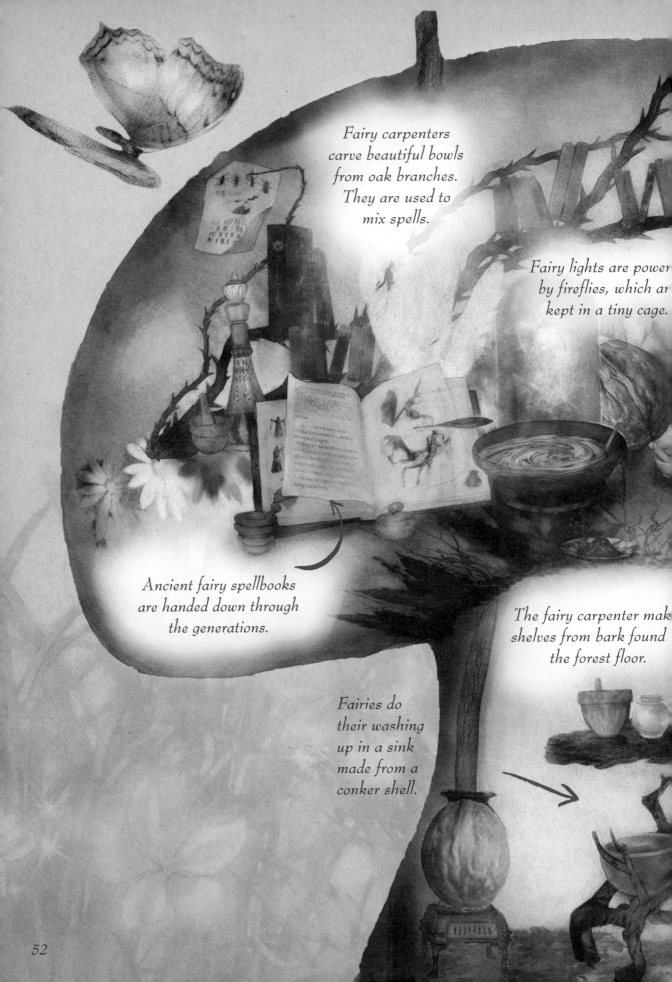

Fairy carpenters carve beautiful bowls from oak branches. They are used to mix spells.

Fairy lights are power by fireflies, which ar kept in a tiny cage.

Ancient fairy spellbooks are handed down through the generations.

The fairy carpenter mak shelves from bark found the forest floor.

Fairies do their washing up in a sink made from a conker shell.

FAIRY FURNISHINGS

Fairy furniture is usually made from natural items such as bark and pebbles. Babies often sleep in a tulip bloom while bigger fairies sleep in leaf and fern beds.

Fairies love preparing delicious meals and entertaining friends and family. They use small toadstools, or stones, as chairs and tables, and tiny bowls and cups are made from nutshells.

Walnut shells are used to hold fairy dust and must be kept locked at all times!

Tiny toadstools can be used as a table and chairs.

Dew-drop showers are made with a system of leaves that collects water from outside to bring into the house.

Most fairies are not very vain but when they need to look at their reflection they use a bowl of water as a mirror.

Comfortable cushions are made from fallen feathers and sewn together with gossamer threads.

DAINTY
DECORATIONS

Fairies are delicate creatures and as you'd expect, the decorations in their homes are as pretty as they are themselves. They use the best silks and threads from their insect friends to weave shimmering fabrics and collect the softest feathers to create cushions to snuggle into.

Should you ever spot a delicate down feather lying on the ground, hide yourself away nearby and watch to see if a fairy skips by to collect it.

FINDING FAIRIES

You may already have fairies at the bottom of your garden or even in your house, but they are very shy creatures and use magic to hide themselves from humans. If you are very lucky, though, you might find clues that a fairy has left behind. Children are much better at spotting these signs than grown-ups. Keep your eyes and ears open, and who knows what you might find.

FAIRY RINGS

At night, fairies have been spotted dancing in woodlands where they leave small circles known as fairy rings. Never go in search of these night-time dancers on your own – their magic can be very powerful. The enchanting music tempts people to come close, but you must always watch from afar. People who have been lured too close to fairy rings have told strange stories of how the dance seemed to last only for a few moments, when in fact they disappeared from their human lives for a whole seven years!

If you see a fairy ring,

In a field of grass,

Very lightly step around,

Tiptoe as you pass;

Last night fairies frolicked there,

And they're sleeping somewhere near.

WILLIAM SHAKESPEARE

SIGNS CLOSE TO HOME

IN THE HOUSE

House fairies are extremely tidy creatures so they are careful to clear up any signs of their presence. But sometimes a little drop of milk or breadcrumbs in the kitchen means the fairies have been having a meal just moments ago.

When your cat seems very interested in something under the cupboard, or the dog seems restless, it may be because they have seen a fairy. If an animal starts chasing its tail, it may be because it has an invisible rider!

SIGNS IN THE GARDEN

Look under the bushes in the garden and see if you
can find a pile of leaves or petals. A fairy may have
slept there. A row or a circle of stones can mean a
midnight meeting has taken place, as they are often
used as seats.

WANDER IN THE WOODS

The most obvious sign that fairies are living in the
woods is a ring of toadstools. Dances and meetings
take place where fairy rings are marked and
toadstools make perfect fairy seats! If you find a
hollow tree, take a peek inside. Any piles of leaves,
acorns or twigs may well have been left there by
fairies making it their home.

ATTRACTING FAIRIES

The best time to attract good fairies is when the
moon is full. This is a very magical time.

Some flowers have special properties. Sunflowers,
nasturtiums and tulips are all garden fairy favourites,
and are likely to draw them near. Fruits, such as
strawberries provide them with food, while sweet-
smelling flowers, such as lavender and honeysuckle,
will attract fairies from far away. Building a fairy
house and leaving tiny cups of water inside is a lovely
way of making the fairies feel welcome.

The best possible way of attracting house fairies is
to keep everything clean! Untidy bedrooms will have
these fairies scooting off into the night, and dust and
dirt will only attract bad fairies. Leave tiny portions of
honey, milk and cake on your windowsill.

BUILDING A FAIRY HOME

Gather together natural materials from the garden or woodland. Twigs, stones, wood, feathers and pine cones all make perfect building materials. Be careful not to pick anything that is living or break any branches. Fairies get very cross if you destroy nature's treasures!

Find a tree, a rock or a wall which you can stack sticks against to make a shelter, and then cover it up with leaves or bark. Stones and shells can be used to make a path or a floor. To invite the fairies in, leave a thimble or acorn full of water and perhaps a tiny piece of cake.

Good luck, spotters.
We hope you attract a
fairy friend!